FOR JO

This edition published 1990
by Guild Publishing
by arrangement with
Walker Books Ltd

First printed 1990
Printed and bound by South China Printing Co. (1988) Ltd

CN 5370

THE
WISH FACTORY
Chris Riddell

GUILD PUBLISHING
LONDON · NEW YORK · SYDNEY · TORONTO

Oliver used to have
a bad dream about a monster.
But one night a cloud came
instead of the dream...

and carried Oliver into
the big, blue night...

far, far away to the Wish Factory.

Oliver closed his eyes and thought a big wish.

Then the wish-makers made
it good and strong...

and wrapped it up to keep it fresh.

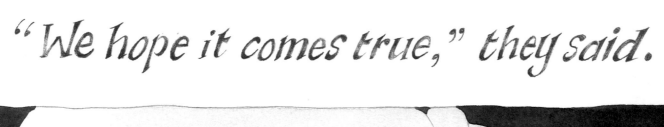

"We hope it comes true," they said.

Then Oliver was in his own bed
and dreaming…

THE BIG BAD DREAM.

So Oliver untied the ribbon...

and out came the wish ...

and the wish came true.

The monster wasn't big
any more, and it wasn't bad.
"Boo!" said Oliver.

And morning came quite soon.